adapted by Christine Ricci
based on the screenplay "Dora's Christmas Carol Adventure" written by Chris Gifford
illustrated by Robert Roper

Simon Spotlight/Nickelodeon
New York London Toronto Sydney

¡Hola! Soy Dora. It's my favorite night of the year. It's *Nochebuena*! That's what I call our Christmas Eve party. The tree is decorated, the picnic tables are full of treats, and all of the presents are under the tree. Everyone in the forest is so excited!

Hey! I see a reindeer sneaking around the Christmas tree. I don't think that's just a reindeer. Who's under that reindeer mask? It's Swiper! Swiper is climbing up the Christmas tree. He's going to swipe the star. Oh, no! If Swiper swipes on Christmas, he'll get on Santa's naughty list!

I hear bells ringing! Do you see anyone in the sky? It's Santa! Look! Santa is using his magic Christmas sparkles to stop Swiper. Santa is saving the party!

Santa put Swiper on the naughty list for trying to swipe the Christmas tree star. To get off the naughty list, Swiper has to travel through time to Christmas in the past, when he was a baby, and to Christmas in the future, when he's older, so he can learn the true spirit of Christmas. We've got to help Swiper! Let's go! *¡Vámonos!*

The Grumpy Old Troll can help us travel through time. But first we have to answer his riddle. Do you know who has a white beard, rides in a sleigh, says "ho, ho, ho," and delivers gifts on Christmas? Santa! We solved the Grumpy Old Troll's riddle and he's giving us capes so we can travel through time.

To travel through time we have to shake our travel capes!

We're in the Christmas Forest of the Past. I see a bunch of babies! Can you guess who the babies are? They are Isa, Tico, Boots, Benny, and even Baby Swiper. Oh, no! Baby Swiper swiped all of the other babies' Christmas presents.

Swiper feels bad that Baby Swiper made all of the babies cry. He's going to return the presents to the babies. I think Swiper is starting to learn the spirit of Christmas.

We traveled through time again, and now we're all little kids. Everyone was playing with their new Christmas toys when Little Kid Swiper swiped all the presents and tossed them into the forest.

Let's help Swiper find all of the toys that Little Kid Swiper swiped. Do you see a toy car for Benny, a bongo drum for Isa, a baseball mitt for Boots, a tricycle for Tico, and a rocking horse for me?

Thanks for helping Swiper find the presents. Swiper's getting the Christmas spirit!

Now we're in the Christmas Forest of the Future, when we're much older. Hey! Do you see an older Dora? Yeah, she's looking at the pine tree, but the tree doesn't have any Christmas decorations on it. Older Swiper swiped everything, and in the future, there won't be a Christmas Eve party at all.

We've got to help Swiper learn the true spirit of Christmas so he won't grow up to be like Older Swiper!

Oh, no! Older Swiper just swiped something else. He took Swiper's travel cape. Without the cape, Swiper can't travel back home!

Luckily, I know some friends who can help! Do you see Older Boots, Benny, Isa, and Tico? They want to help us get the cape back.

We've got to find Older Swiper, but we don't know where he went. Who do we ask for help when we don't know which way to go? Map! Map says that the wrapping-paper trail leads to the castle where Older Swiper lives. Do you see the wrapping-paper trail? Let's go!

We made it to the castle. Do you see Older Swiper? Yeah! He's asleep in his rocking chair. Older Swiper looks lonely.

Swiper doesn't want to end up all alone on Christmas without any friends. He really wants to learn the true spirit of Christmas.

We need to find the purple traveling cape so Swiper can get home. Look around the castle. Do you see the purple traveling cape? You found it! Let's travel back home. *¡Vámonos!*

We made it home just in time for Santa to deliver our Christmas presents. Santa has presents for everyone except Swiper. He is still on the naughty list.

Instead of getting presents, Swiper has something that he wants to give us. What is Swiper giving us? It's his bunny. Swiper is giving it to us to thank us for helping him today.

Bells are ringing! Swiper has learned the true spirit of Christmas: It is better to give than to receive . . . or to swipe!

Swiper is no longer on the naughty list! Santa gives Swiper a bag full of presents and Swiper is giving all of his presents away. We helped Swiper learn the true spirit of Christmas. We did it! *¡Feliz Navidad!* Merry Christmas!